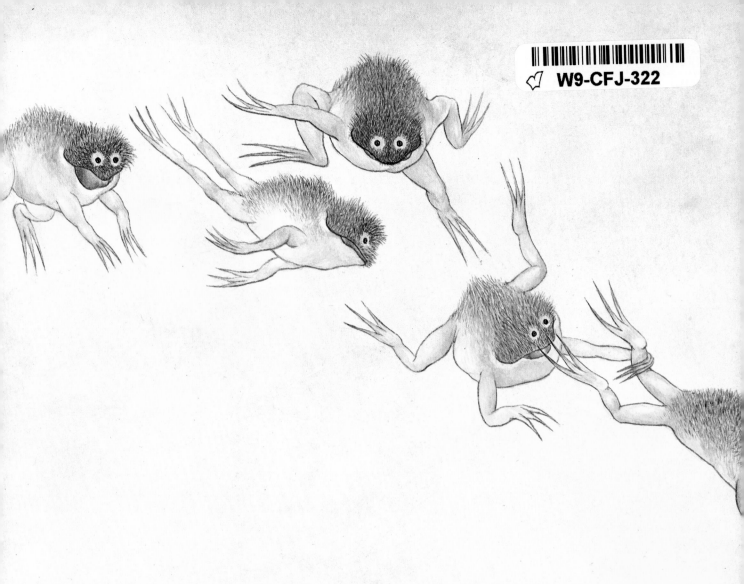

W9-CFJ-322

First American Edition 1985 by Kane/Miller Book Publishers
Brooklyn, New York & La Jolla, California

Originally published in the Netherlands under the title *Helemaal
verkikkerd*. Copyright © 1981 Limniscaat b.v. Rotterdam
American text copyright © 1985 by Kane/Miller Book Publishers
All rights reserved. For information contact:
Kane/Miller Book Publishers, P.O. Box 529, Brooklyn, N.Y. 11231

Library of Congress Cataloging in Publication Data

Schubert, Ingrid, 1953-
   The magic bubble trip.

   Translation of Helemaal verkikkerd.
   ''A Cranky Nell book.''
   Summary: James blows a giant bubble that carries
   him away to a land of large hairy frogs.
   1. Children's stories, Dutch. [1. Bubbles—Fiction.
   2. Frogs—Fiction] I. Schubert, Dieter, 1947-
   II. Title.
   PZ7.S3834Mag 1985   [E]   84-25071
   ISBN 0-916291-02-2
   ISBN 0-916291-03-0 (pbk.)

Printed and bound in Tokyo by Dai Nippon Printing Company

2   3   4   5   6   7   8   9   10

Ingrid & Dieter Schubert

The Magic Bubble Trip

A CRANKY NELL BOOK

Kane/Miller Book Publishers

Brooklyn, New York & La Jolla, California

James lives in a big apartment building. The woods behind the building, however, are where James can usually be found, for in the woods is a pond full of frogs. And James loves frogs.

One Saturday morning when James comes back home from the pond,
he sneaks into the bathroom and locks the door. Soon there is the sound
of running water and after that a strange noise. Ploop . . . ploop . . .
ploop . . . ploop.

"What's going on in there?" asks James' father.

James' father and mother haven't the foggiest idea. His mother peeks
through the keyhole.

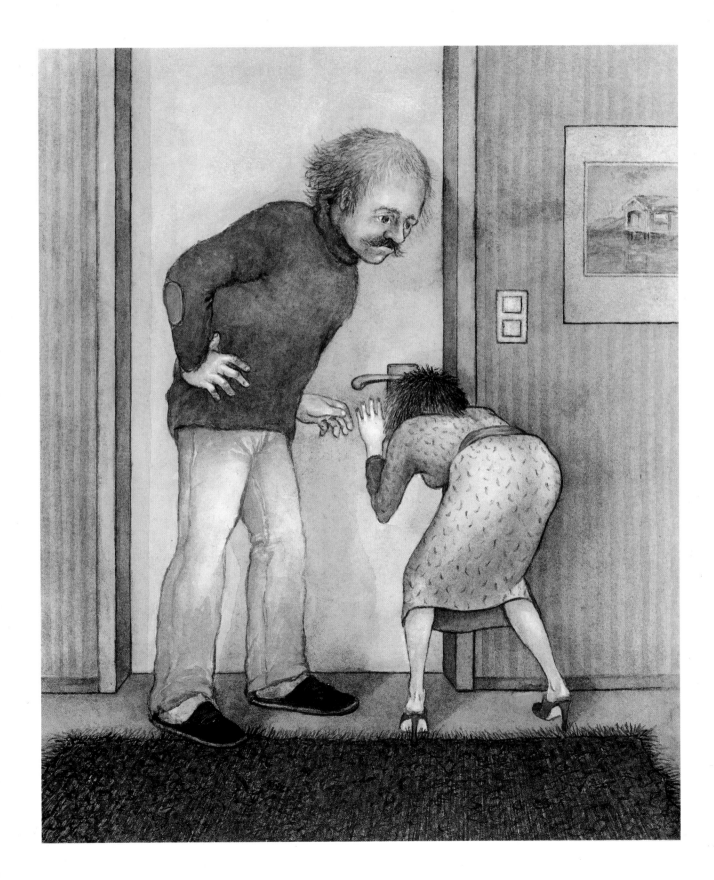

She sees James playing with his frogs. One at a time, he places the frogs on his head. And then, taking turns, the frogs leap from the top of James' head into the bathtub filled with water. Ploop.

"Goodness James!" his parents cry out. "An apartment is no place for frogs. They belong in the woods—in a pond. Not in a house."

"But they like it here. I know they do."

His parents, however, insist he return the frogs to the pond immediately.

Back in his room James is feeling very sad, for he misses his frog friends. He sits on his bed blowing soap bubbles, as he usually does when something bothers him. He daydreams, thinking of frogs and other things.

Just then, something strange happens. Something very strange.

One of the soap bubbles begins to grow bigger and bigger and bigger. When it has grown so large that the bubble completely surrounds James, it starts to float out the apartment window, carrying him along with it.

At first James is afraid, but he soon begins to enjoy the bubble ride, for he can see everything. The bubble floats high above the streets and trees—higher even than James' apartment building.

He floats on and on. Finally the bubble begins to float downward. Below him James sees a meadow with mysterious looking mounds in it. It is here that the bubble gently lands.

Up close James sees that the mounds are really hundreds of grassy frogs piled on top of each other. And as the frogs jump out to greet James, the mounds disappear.

"Hello, hello," croak the giant frogs. "Who are you?"

"I'm James. But why do you make these piles of yourselves, and why do you have grass on your backs and on your heads?"

"We pile up high on top of one another so that we can get a better view," say the frogs. "And as for the grass? Well, we have grass because we're grass frogs! And anyway, you have grass on the top of your head too, even it it is all dried up."

"That's not grass," laughs James. "That's my hair!"

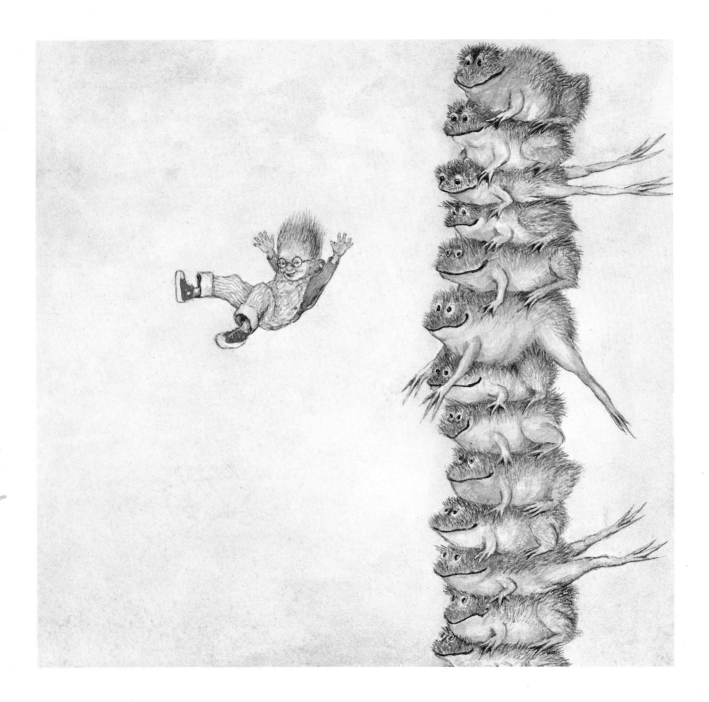

Soon James is playing all kinds of games with the grass frogs, who, it turns out, are extremely playful. The game he likes best is when the frogs sit on top of each other to make a high tower, and then he climbs to the top and jumps down. James does this at least twenty times, laughing each time as he lands in the grass.

"Now I'll show you something," James says, and he begins to jump about on one leg. The grass frogs try to copy him, but they are used to jumping on four legs and find it very difficult to jump on just one.

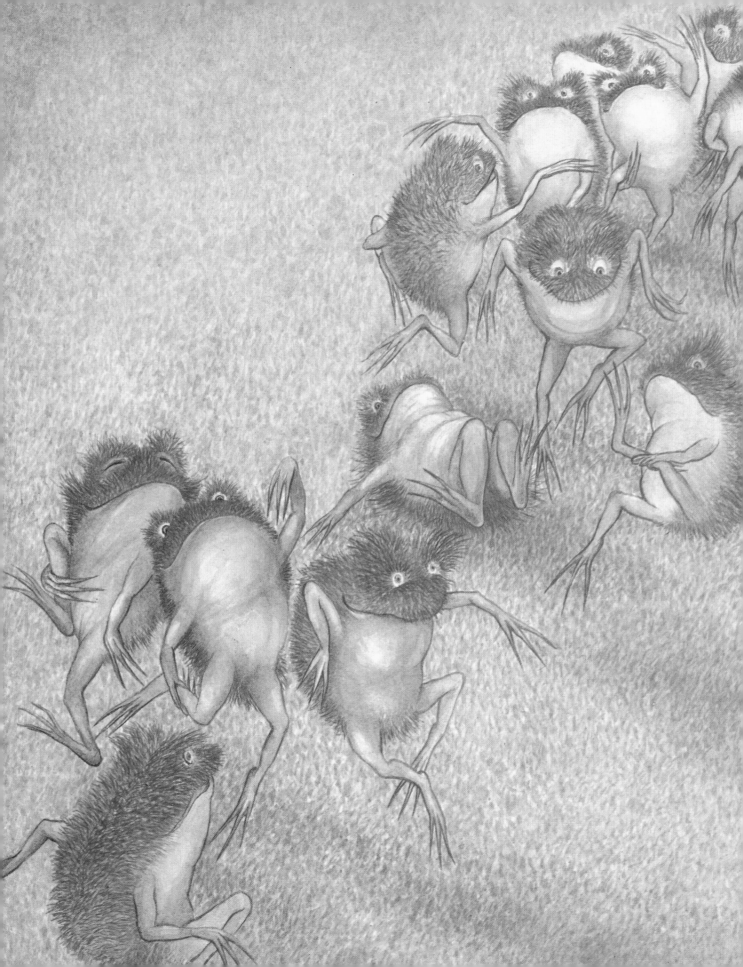

While James jumps up and down, things fall out of his pockets: a screwdriver, soap for blowing bubbles, a wing nut, a spoon (a little bit bent), an old nail (a little bit bent too), a button and all sorts of other objects.

"What are those?" the grass frogs ask.

"They're just things I save. Odds and ends that might come in handy someday."

"Then we bet you'd like to meet our friend Mr. Odds-and-Ends," say the frogs. "He collects old stuff just like you do."

"I'd love to meet him," says James.

He blows a bubble just big enough for himself and one grass frog, who goes along to show him the way. They float until the grass frog tells James to land near what seems to be an enormous junkyard.

Next to the junkyard is a colorful but very funny-looking house. From inside the house James hears the sound of hammering. He walks over to see what's going on.

"Are you Mr. Odds-and-Ends?" James asks.

"That's me all right! But who are you?"

"I'm James."

"Well then, come on in James," Mr. Odds-and-Ends says with a smile.

Inside James is delighted to see a room full of wonderful toys. Mr. Odds-and-Ends has constructed them himself out of this and that, and he tells James exactly what materials he used to make each one. The toy James likes the best is a grass frog made from matchboxes, buttons and green wool.

"If you like these, then let me show you the best thing of all," says Mr. Odds-and-Ends, and he takes James to a large shed behind the house.

"Here it is. My Heli-plane. The only problem is that before it can fly I need one very small part to tighten its left wing. I've looked all through the junk pile but haven't been able to find the part anywhere."

"How about this?" James asks, showing Mr. Odds-and-Ends the wing nut from his pocket.

"That's it! That's it!" Mr. Odds-and-Ends cries. "That's what it needs to fly." He takes the wing nut from James, and as a thank you gives him the matchbox grass frog.

"Come on,
let's take a
ride," Mr. Odds-
and-Ends says to James
after he finishes tightening
the wing. "I'll take you back
home in the Heli-plane."

"Great," says James, who climbs aboard
after saying goodbye to his giant grass frog
friend. The giant grass frog doesn't join them, for
there is not enough room in the Heli-plane, and, anyway, he must return to his own home in the land of the
frogs. But James does take the toy matchbox frog.

The Heli-plane flies beautifully. Mr. Odds-and-Ends is an expert
pilot. He does loop the loops and other flying tricks until at last they
arrive at James' home. Stairs extend out from the Heli-plane to the
windowsill of the apartment. After saying goodbye and thank you to Mr.
Odds-and-Ends, James walks down the stairs, onto the sill and into his house.

Waiting inside for James is the biggest surprise of his life. His parents, who before never wanted frogs in the house, are now playing cheerfully on the floor with several giant grass frogs.

A big smile breaks out on James' face. He cannot believe his eyes. He has never felt happier.

Sometimes life can seem wonderful, he thinks. Sometimes it can almost seem too good to be true!